Oh, Rats!

By Dona Herweck Rice
Illustrated by Sholto Walker

Mom is beautiful.

Just look at her!

There is no one in the world as beautiful as she is.

Her coat is rough and gray.

Her teeth are long and yellow.

Her eyes are small and pink.

She looks a little sneaky.

Mom gets her good looks from Grandpa.

Grandpa has the longest, yellowest teeth.

Wow! He is one handsome rat.

All the rats say so.

Grandma and Grandpa had about four thousand babies.

But Mom is the prettiest of the whole bunch.

When I grow up, I hope I look just like her.

The thing is, Mom is really smart too.

I think she gets that from Grandma.

A scientist once put Grandma
in a maze.

She had to find the cheese.

No problem!

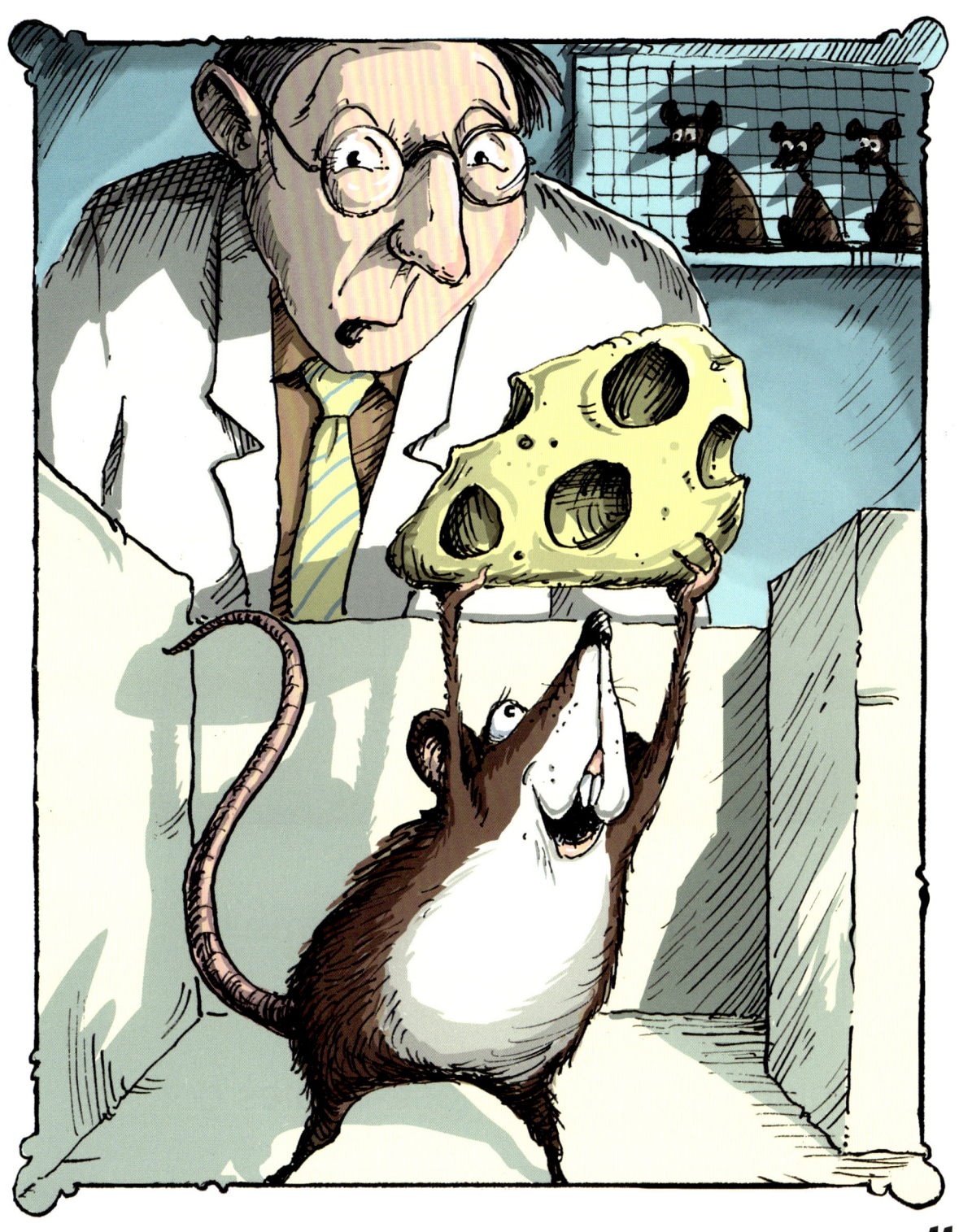

I think Grandma liked her time in the maze.

Taking care of all those babies got pretty tiring!

The maze was like a little vacation for her.

Of course, Grandpa also took care of the kids.

He's much more than a handsome face, you know!

We all live together.

There is Mom, Dad, Grandma, Grandpa, and me.

All my brothers and sisters live here too.

There are many aunts, uncles, and cousins as well.

Really, it is hard to tell how many of us are here.

New babies are born every day!

We are just one big happy rat family!

Consultant

Doug Dalton, M.A.Ed.
Elementary Teacher
Sierra Sands Unified School District, California

Publishing Credits

Rachelle Cracchiolo, M.S.Ed., *Publisher*
Emily R. Smith, M.A.Ed., *VP of Content Development*
Véronique Bos, *Creative Director*

Image Credits:
Illustrated by Sholto Walker

Library of Congress Cataloging-in-Publication Data

Names: Rice, Dona, author. | Walker, Sholto, illustrator.
Title: Oh, rats! / by Dona Herweck Rice ; illustrated by Sholto Walker.
Description: Huntington Beach, CA : Teacher Created Materials, [2022] | Includes book club questions. | Audience: Grades K-1.
Identifiers: LCCN 2020006561 (print) | LCCN 2020006562 (ebook) | ISBN 9781087601267 (paperback) | ISBN 9781087619309 (ebook)
Subjects: LCSH: Readers (Primary) | Rats--Juvenile fiction.
Classification: LCC PE1119 .R4659 2020 (print) | LCC PE1119 (ebook) | DDC 428.6/2--dc23
LC record available at https://lccn.loc.gov/2020006561
LC ebook record available at https://lccn.loc.gov/2020006562

5482 Argosy Avenue
Huntington Beach, CA 92649
www.tcmpub.com

ISBN 978-1-0876-0126-7

© 2022 Teacher Created Materials, Inc.

This book may not be reproduced or distributed in any way without prior written consent from the publisher.